MAU, KING OF THE CATS

In this lively book, Mau, King of the Cats, and Pharaoh, King of the people of Memphis, finally come to a long-awaited meeting. Each requires the other's services; the Pharaoh needs Mau and his tribe to wipe out the mice which are ruining his crops, and Mau needs fish and freedom for his tribe at all times. The solution to their problems is depicted in this delightful book.

MISCHA DAMJAN

MAU

King of the Cats

Adapted by Ann McGovern

Illustrated by Werner Büchi

G. P. Putnam's Sons   New York

Many, many years ago there lived a cat who was wise and good. He was King Mau, king of the cats in Egypt, where the River Nile flows. King Mau should have been the happiest of kings, for he loved his tribe and they loved him. But Mau had two big worries — fish and freedom!

Mau and his tribe longed for fat, tasty fish. The River Nile was full of fish. But the River Nile was full of crocodiles too — crocodiles that could snap up cats who hunted in the river.

There *was* a way to get fish, Mau knew. He had heard of the great Pharaoh, king of a nearby city. The Pharaoh's men caught lots of fish. But Mau said, "The Pharaoh is a man! Men put chains on their animals!" Hadn't Mau seen dogs in chains begging for bones? "I will never give up freedom for fish," Mau said. "Never!"

So King Mau and his tribe went hungry.

Mau thought the Pharaoh was a happy man, with so many fish in his kingdom. But this was not true. The great Pharaoh was very sad.

The Pharaoh and his people were hungry. They were tired of living on fish alone. They longed for corn and rice, and grain to make bread. But there was not one kernel of corn or rice or grain left in the entire kingdom. The mice had come!

The mice stole into the fields. They crept into the storerooms. They ate up the rich harvest of the city. They ate and ate until even the Pharaoh's private bins were empty.

The mice had come! So the Pharaoh and his people went hungry.

In Mau's kingdom, the days passed slowly. These were hungry days, fishless days. Sometimes Mau went to the banks of the River Nile to think. He saw crocodiles with snapping jaws. He saw fishermen pull out nets filled with fat fish from the river.

Mau smelled the fish. He wanted the fish so badly he could almost taste them. But then Mau remembered the chained dogs. "I know that the men would give me fish for my tribe," Mau thought. "But the men would also put my tribe in chains. No! I will never give up freedom for fish."

The other kings in Egypt were well fed. "Perhaps they can help me," Mau said.

So he went to see Hyenka, Queen of the hyenas. "Do you have any fish to spare?" Mau asked.

"I am sorry," Hyenka said, "but hyenas do not eat fish."

Then Mau asked Leo, King of the lions. Leo roared. "How the animals in Egypt would laugh to see my powerful lions eating tiny fish. Sorry, Mau, but I cannot help you."

One night Mau and his hunters prowled to the Pharaoh's gate to get a better sniff of the delicious fish. They heard the guards whispering.

"I am so hungry," said one.

"I am so sick of fish!" said the other.

Mau couldn't believe his ears. The Pharaoh's tribe hungry? The Pharaoh's tribe sick of fish? Impossible!

The next day Mau saw some of the Pharaoh's men. "Where are you going?" he called from a safe distance.

"We are going to find food," they answered. "The mice have eaten our last corn. All we have left is fish."

Mau licked his lips. "Mice, too, would be good to eat," he thought. "The Pharaoh needs me and my hunters."

But once more a picture of the chained dogs flashed through his mind. "No, not even for fish *and* mice will I give up freedom!" he said.

The Pharaoh watched the men leave the city.

"Soon there will be no one left except me and these horrible mice," he said sadly. "What I need is —"

He snapped his fingers. "WHAT I NEED IS CATS!"

The very next day, the Pharaoh's chariots rolled across the desert, racing toward the Kingdom of the Cats.

The Pharaoh's messengers saluted and bowed to King Mau and his tribe.

King Mau and his tribe bowed back — from a safe distance.

Three Egyptian messengers stepped forward. "The mighty Pharaoh requests your presence at the palace." they said.

"Oh," said Mau. "This is a most serious request. I shall have to call a meeting to discuss it."

And so while Mau and his wise cats held their council, the Pharaoh's messengers pitched their tents and waited for Mau's answer.

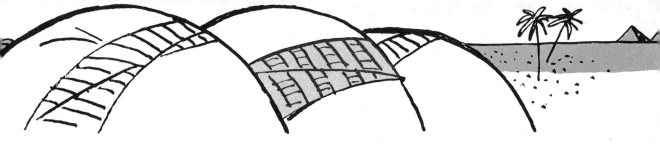

The next day Mau told the Egyptians, "We have reached a decision. We shall come in three days. Tell your Pharaoh that when the sun rises on the third day, I shall pass through the gates of your city."

Three big Egyptians bowed gratefully before little Mau.

When the sun rose on the third day, Mau and his
hunters stalked through the Pharaoh's gates.

The people looked at them with hungry eyes and
thought of cat stew. But no one dared to touch them.
The Pharaoh had given his orders!

The smell of fish became stronger as the cats climbed the steps of the palace.

"The Pharaoh is a clever king," Mau thought. "He tempts me with fish. But to me, freedom is far more tempting."

Mau and his hunters were shown into the Pharaoh's private chambers.

The Pharaoh did not waste any time.

"Mau," he said, "if your tribe fights the mice in my kingdom, you may have anything you desire."

"Anything?" Mau asked. "Can it be two things?"

"Two things, if it pleases you," the Pharaoh said.

"Very well," said Mau. "We want fish and freedom, freedom and fish."

The Pharaoh smiled and said, "Agreed. You will have your fish. And you will have your freedom. No one will tie you to a chain. We will draw up a pact immediately."

He snapped his fingers. His Secretary came running in with a long scroll under his arm.

Thus a pact was drawn up between Pharaoh, King of the people and Mau, King of the cats.

The Pharaoh's messengers saddled their fastest horses and galloped from village to village.

"The Pharaoh and Mau have pledged everlasting friendship," they shouted.

"Mau and his tribe will drive away the mice," they shouted even louder.

With their tails raised high, Mau and his tribe went to work. The people cheered wildly.

But the mice ran for their lives. They hid in their deepest holes. And from one hole to the other, they whispered fearfully, "*Psst!* The Great Enemy is here! We are lost!"

Once again there was plenty of bread in Egypt. The Egyptians ate and ate and grew tall and strong and smart. They built huge pyramids. And they became leaders in arithmetic and drawing, too.

And Mau and his tribe had fish. They ate fish to their hearts' content and grew big and strong.

Mau and his tribe had freedom, too. And one day they strolled out into the world . . .

So whenever a cat crosses your path, remember that he is descended from clever Mau. Give him fish, give him freedom.

And he will be a most contented cat!

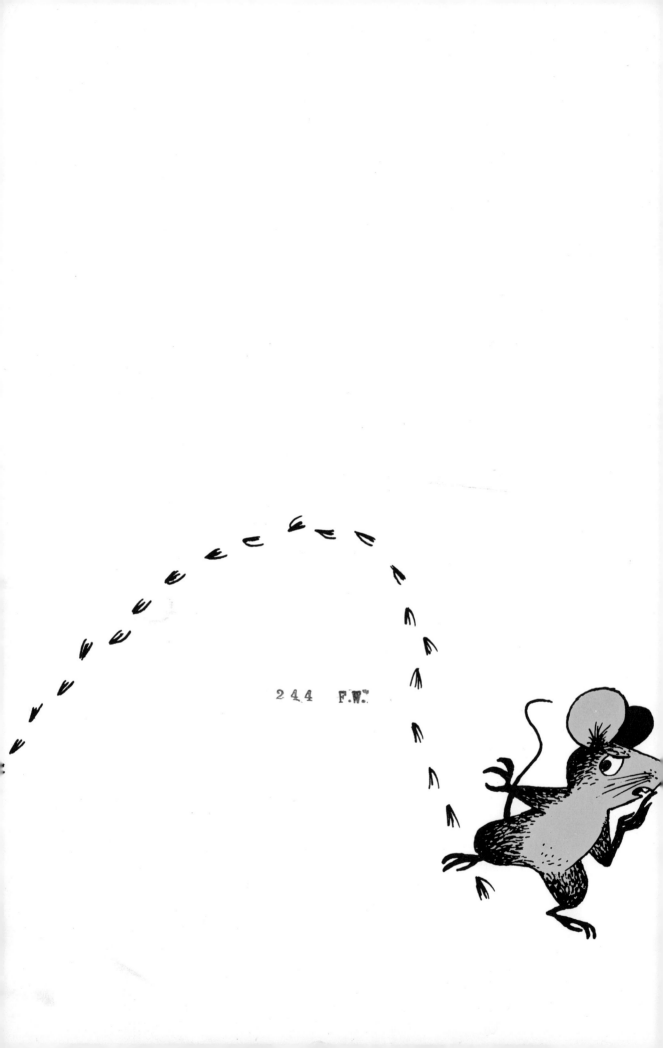

244 F.W.